Querido dragón quiere ayudar

Dear Dragon Helps Out

por/by Margaret Hillert
ilustrado por/Illustrated by David Schimmell

NORWOOD HOUSE PRESS

Queridos padres y maestros:

La serie para lectores principiantes es una colección de lecturas cuidadosamente escritas, muchas de las cuales ustedes recordarán de su propia infancia. Cada libro comprende palabras de uso frecuente en español e inglés y, a través de la repetición, le ofrece al niño la oportunidad de practicarlas. Los detalles adicionales de las ilustraciones refuerzan la historia y le brindan la oportunidad de ayudar a su niño a desarrollar el lenguaje oral y la comprensión.

Primero, léale el cuento al niño; después deje que él lea las palabras con las que está familiarizado y pronto, podrá leer solito todo el cuento. En cada paso, elogie el esfuerzo del niño para que se sienta más confiado como lector independiente. Hable sobre las ilustraciones y anime al niño a relacionar el cuento con su propia vida.

Sobre todo, la parte más importante de la experiencia de la lectura es ¡divertirse y disfrutarla!

Shannon Cannon

Shannon Cannon
Consultora de lectoescritura

Dear Caregiver,

The *Beginning-to-Read* series is a carefully written collection of readers, many of which you may remember from your own childhood. This book, *Dear Dragon's Day with Father*, was written over 30 years after the first *Dear Dragon* books were published. The *New Dear Dragon* series features the same elements of the earlier books, such as text comprised of common sight words. These sight words provide your child with ample practice reading the words that appear most frequently in written text. The many additional details in the pictures enhance the story and offer the opportunity for you to help your child expand oral language skills and develop comprehension.

Begin by reading the story to your child, followed by letting him or her read familiar words and soon your child will be able to read the story independently. At each step of the way, be sure to praise your reader's efforts to build his or her confidence as an independent reader. Discuss the pictures and encourage your child to make connections between the story and his or her own life.

Above all, the most important part of the reading experience is to have fun and enjoy it!

Shannon Cannon

Shannon Cannon,
Literacy Consultant

Norwood House Press • P.O. Box 316598 • Chicago, Illinois 60631
For more information about Norwood House Press please visit our website at
www.norwoodhousepress.com or call 866-565-2900.
Text copyright ©2014 by Margaret Hillert. Illustrations and cover design copyright ©2014 by
Norwood House Press, Inc. All rights reserved. No part of this book may be reproduced or utilized
in any form or by any means without written permission from the publisher.
Designer: The Design Lab

LIBRARY OF CONGRESS CATALOGING-IN-PUBLICATION DATA
  Hillert, Margaret.
   Querido dragón quiere ayudar = Dear dragon helps out / por Margaret
  Hillert ; ilustrado por David Schimmell ; traducido por Queta Fernandez.
      pages cm. -- (A beginning-to-read book)
   Summary: "A boy and his pet dragon find the joy in being helpful to
  others"-- Provided by publisher.
   ISBN 978-1-59953-613-2 (library edition : alk. paper) -- ISBN
  978-1-60357-621-5 (ebook)
  [1. Helpfulness--Fiction. 2. Dragons--Fiction. 3. Spanish language
  materials--Bilingual.] I. Schimmell, David, illustrator. II. Fernandez,
  Queta, translator. III. Hillert, Margaret. Querido dragón quiere ayudar.
  Spanish. IV. Hillert, Margaret. Dear dragon helps out. V. Title. VI. Title:
  Dear dragon helps out.
   PZ73.H5572084 2014
   [E]--dc23
                                                         2013034959

Manufactured in the United States of America in Brainerd, Minnesota.
240N—012014

Mamá, mamá.	Mother, Mother.
No tengo nada que hacer.	I have nothing to do.
¿Qué puedo hacer?	What can I do?

3

Eso no es bueno.
Es bueno tener
algo que hacer.

That is not good.
It is good to have
something to do.

4

Eh. Mira allá afuera.
Es una amiga.
Creo que te necesita.

Oh, look out here.
It's a friend.
I guess she wants you.

Aquí estoy.
¿En qué puedo ayudarte?

Here I am.
How can I help you?

¿Puedes llevar a mi perro a pasear?
A él le gusta caminar.

Can you take my dog for a walk?
He likes to walk.

Sí. Vamos, perro.
Daremos un paseo largo y agradable.

Yes. Come on, dog.
We will take a good, long walk.

8

Allí hay un gatito marrón.
¿Dónde está la mamá?

There is a little brown baby cat.
Where is the mother?

Ah, allí está. Quieto, perro, quieto.
No saltes. No tenemos que ayudar.
La mamá ayudará al bebé.

Oh, there she is. Down, dog, down.
Do not jump. We do not have to help.
The mother will help the baby.

Vamos, perro.
Te llevaré a casa.

Come on now, dog.
I will take you home.

Ahora puedo trabajar contigo, papá.
Puedo poner las hojas en la bolsa.

Now I can do work for you, Father.
I can get these leaves in the bag.

Qué hojas tan lindas,
hojas rojas y amarillas.

What pretty leaves.
Red and yellow leaves.

Es divertido jugar aquí,
pero tenemos que trabajar.
¿Quieres ayudar también?

It is fun to play here.
but we have to work.
Do you want to help too?

Sí. Yo puedo ayudar.
Luego podemos ir allí y jugar.

Yes. I can help.
Then we can go over there and play.

Sí, sí.
Será divertido.

Yes, yes.
That will be fun.

¡Caramba!
¡Qué bien lo haces!

Boy!
You are good at this.

Tú también eres muy bueno.
¡Somos un buen equipo!

You are pretty good too.
We make a good team!

Fue divertido,
pero quiero ir a comer algo.

That was fun.
But I want to go and eat something.

Iré contigo.

I will go with you.

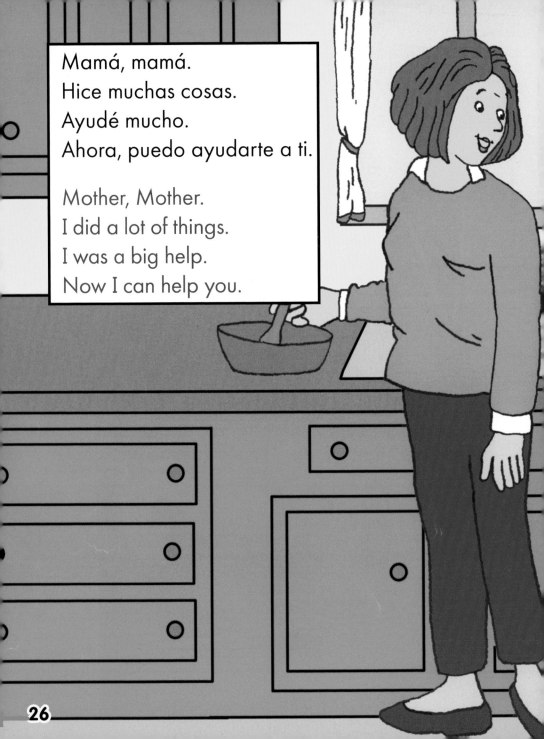

Mamá, mamá.
Hice muchas cosas.
Ayudé mucho.
Ahora, puedo ayudarte a ti.

Mother, Mother.
I did a lot of things.
I was a big help.
Now I can help you.

Oh, querido dragón, yo estoy contigo.
Tú estás conmigo.
Qué bueno es tener amigos.

Oh dear dragon, here I am with you.
Here you are with me.
It is so good to have friends.

READING REINFORCEMENT

The following activities support the findings of the National Reading Panel that determined the most effective components for reading instruction are: Phonemic Awareness, Phonics, Vocabulary, Fluency, and Text Comprehension.

Phonemic Awareness: The /h/ sound

Deletion: Ask your child to say the following words without the beginning /**h**/ sound:

hat - /h/ = at	hop - /h/ = op	ham - /h/ = am
hit - /h/ = it	his - /h/ = is	harm - /h/ = arm
hand - /h/ = and	hair - /h/ = air	

Phonics: The letter Hh

1. Demonstrate how to form the letters **H** and **h** for your child.

2. Have your child practice writing **H** and **h** at least three times each.

3. Ask your child to point to the words in the book that start with the letter **h**.

4. Write down the following words and ask your child to circle the letter **h** in each word:

happy	hand	mother	hug
help	father	home	how
hair	the	there	here
hut	house	where	have

Vocaubulary: Baby Animal Names

1. Explain to your child that baby animals often have different names than their parents.

2. Write each of the following words on separate index cards:

rabbit/bunny	squirrel/pup	skunk/kit	tiger/cub
frog/tadpole	cow/calf	pig/piglet	dog/puppy
cat/kitten	duck/duckling	chicken/chick	goat/kid
goose/gosling	kangaroo/joey	deer/fawn	horse/foal

3. Place the adult and baby names next to each other and read the words to your child.

4. Mix up the words.

5. Work with your child to match the adult/baby animal pairs.

Fluency: Choral Reading

1. Reread the story to your child at least two more times while your child tracks the print by running a finger under the words as they are read. Ask your child to read the words he or she knows with you.

2. Reread the story aloud together. Be careful to read at a rate that your child can keep up with.

3. Repeat choral reading and allow your child to be the lead reader and ask him or her to change from a whisper to a loud voice while you follow along and change your voice.

Text Comprehension: Discussion Time

1. Ask your child to retell the sequence of events in the story.

2. To check comprehension, ask your child the following questions:

   • What are some of the things that the boy did to help other people?

   • Why do you think the cat did not need help with the baby cat?

   • What do the boy and his friend do when they are finished working?

   • What are some things that you do to help other people?

ACERCA DE LA AUTORA

Margaret Hillert ha escrito más de 80 libros para niños que están aprendiendo a leer. Sus libros han sido traducidos a muchos idiomas y han sido leídos por más de un millón de niños de todo el mundo. De niña, Margaret empezó escribiendo poesía y más adelante siguió escribiendo para niños y adultos. Durante 34 años, fue maestra de primer grado. Ya se retiró, y ahora vive en Michigan donde le gusta escribir, dar paseos matinales y cuidar a sus tres gatos.

ABOUT THE AUTHOR

Margaret Hillert has written over 80 books for children who are just learning to read. Her books have been translated into many different languages and over a million children throughout the world have read her books. She first started writing poetry as a child and has continued to write for children and adults throughout her life. A first grade teacher for 34 years, Margaret is now retired from teaching and lives in Michigan where she likes to write, take walks in the morning, and care for her three cats.

ACERCA DEL ILUSTRADOR

David Schimmell fue bombero durante 23 años, al cabo de los cuales guardó las botas y el casco y se dedicó a trabajar como ilustrador. David ha creado las ilustraciones para la nueva serie de Querido dragón, así como para muchos otros libros. David nació y se crió en Evansville, Indiana, donde aún vive con su esposa, dos hijos, un nieto y dos nietas.

ABOUT THE ILLUSTRATOR

David Schimmell served as a professional firefighter for 23 years before hanging up his boots and helmet to devote himself to work as an illustrator. David has happily created the illustrations for the New Dear Dragon books as well as many other books throughout his career. Born and raised in Evansville, Indiana, he lives there today with his wife, two sons, a grandson and two granddaughters.